S.E.X.

SuccessEnergyXxx©

*What Males really know
about Females?
And
what do you have to
know?*

Thanks to all of our inspiration givers, we hope, we can help you all a bit and you will smile a bit more!

Authors Tips:

Just do it and smile.
Be grateful for all bad and good things in your life,
BE GRATEFUL FOR YOUR LIFE.

Say thank you to your life, every day, just say it!
And the life will be Grateful to you!
Don't think to much.

Keep
Calm.

Smile.

S.E.X.

SuccessEnergyXxx©
P.S. MinimalismArt

What Males really know
about Females?
And
What do you have to know?

Motivation Minimalism and Fun Art©

Impressum / Imprint:

© 2017 S.E.X. Success Energy Xxx /
P.S.MinimalismArt

Herstellung und Verlag: BoD – Books on Demand
GmbH, Norderstedt
Alle urheberrelevanten Rechte wie
Umschlaggestaltung, Satz, Layout, Bildverwendung
usw. liegen beim Autor.

Illustration:
S.E.X., Motivation Minimalism and Fun Art©

1.Auflage
ISBN: 978-3-7448-8894-3

Bibliografische informationen der Deutschen
Nationalbibliothek:
Die Deutsche Nationalbibliothek verzeichnet diese
Publikation in der Deutschen Nationalbibliografie;
Bibliografische Daten sind im Internet über
http/dnb.d-nb.de abrufbar

Table of Contents

Chapter1 – About the Authors:

1. Author:
S.E.X.:

She loves to motivate people to do what they
want to do.
(Like: go and start your training, business,…
now.)
She loves it to speak and write.
She tries to spread more Love, Fun, Energy,
Motivation, Peace and XXX in the World.

Her tips:
Just do it, make Love and keep Calm.

2. Author:
P.S. MinimalismArt:

He likes to motivate people to do what they
want to do.
(Like: take your time and breath.)
He likes to inform people in a practical short
time-saving manner and minimalism-art.

His tip:
Say everyday thanks to life and Smile.

Chapter2 – What Males really know about Females?

Males main knowledge about Females:

Females are Female, need water, good food and

and

and

Good

Females are allowed to drink a bit!

.That's also important…

!!!!!!!!!!!!!!!!

and

but

So Lovely.

so good.

That was a lot of information but very important!

Chapter2 – The secrets about Males knowlege 1.0:

.And

and

Now will follow the second part.

Chapter4 – The secrets about Males knowlege 1.1:

Maybe it is copied from Hollywood-films.

Otherwise

But also

Not so easy

and it will be good!

Really lovely

That was a lot. So breath and start with the next Chapter!

Chapter5 – What can you know? What do you have to know?

Female

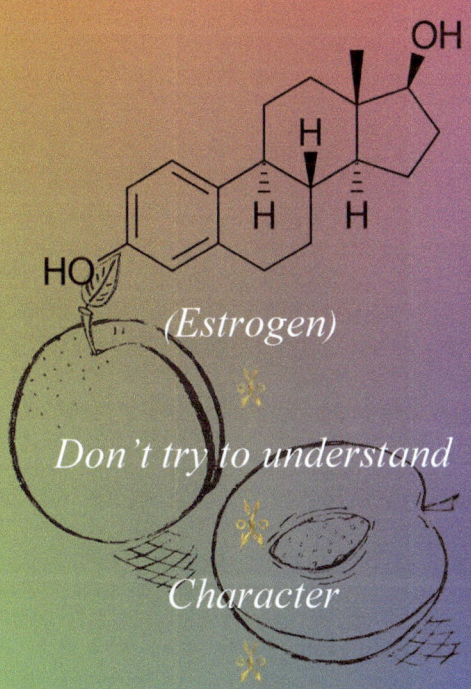

(Estrogen)

Don't try to understand

Character

Don't be a Pussy.

Keep Calm

Smile.

Chapter6 – Extra knowledge

Try to have a lil bit more fun with people around you, make them laugh or smile, wherever you are but don't be a clown. (it's too odd ;))

If you're shy person: (the gender dosen't matter.)

Keep calm and
Smile.

Smile every day!
If you smile and the other person smile too just say:
,, Hey'' or ,, How are
you?''. Aaaand keep
smiling!!
But not like a psycho made in the darkest nightmare, do it naturally l ike:
,,ooohhhh there is a flying Unimingorn*, over the rainbow, under the warm shining sun, riding some golden ravens!''......

*Illustration at the last Page.

...Do it every day and say every day
thank you to lif e.
Trust in life and stay in presence, not
in past or future.
If your mind is in past or in future the
time will be uncertain.
By the way:
Both, past and future are not real, u can't
change your past stories and you
can't see the future.
Stay in presence.
Live for the moment,
speak less, do more!
Just the moment now is real, nothing
else!!

And smile!

And your life will be a lil bit better
than before!

Now you know Males secret
knowledge about female like:

and

and

and

and

and...

like

love

Do it and...

Sooo time for the Chapter! next

*Kiss
Someone, for
example, the
next person
you will see!*

Chapter 7 – Sex, Tips and Inspiration

Make Love

Feel Love

Be Honest

Feel Sex

Enjoy Sex

But always Safety first

Use Condoms

Keep Calm

Smile

I scream so mad
Ice-cream!

LICK SOME
ICE-CREAM

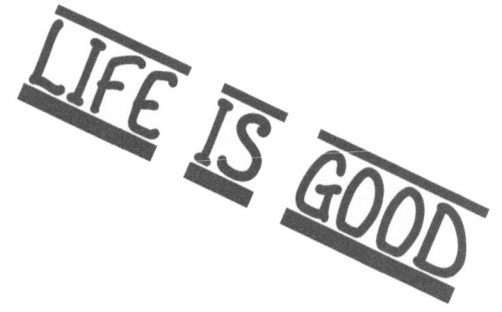

And

LOVE

We hope you enjoyed this litte funny minimalism art of a book.

Now you know almost all secrets that males know about Females.

The next minimalism art of a book will follow:

Motivation, fun and some very important tips for wealth and health?
In a good and time-saving manner.

Much love, stay tuned.

Your Authors, Artists, Motivators and Lovers:
S.E.X. and P.S. MinimalismArt
by Motivation Minimalism   and Fun art.

*here is the
image of
the
mysterium
from page
111:

Unimingorn©
by S.E.X.